The Catfish Club

Purrmaids

2

The Catfish Club

by Sudipta Bardhan-Quallen

illustrations by Vivien Wu

SCHOLASTIC INC.

ISBN 978-1-338-27280-2

Text copyright © 2017 by Sudipta Bardhan-Quallen. Cover art copyright © 2017 by Andrew Farley. Illustrations copyright © 2017 by Vivien Wu. All rights reserved. Published by Scholastic Inc., 557 Broadway, New York, NY 10012, by arrangement with Random House Children's Books, a division of Penguin Random House LLC. PURRMAIDS® is a registered trademark of KIKIDOODLE LLC and is used under license from KIKIDOODLE LLC. SCHOLASTIC and associated logos are trademarks and/or registered trademarks of Scholastic Inc.

12 11 10 9 8 7 6 5   18 19 20 21 22 23

Printed in the U.S.A.   40

First Scholastic printing, January 2018

To my favorite artist, Brooklyn Quallen

1

Angel loved almost everything about living in Kittentail Cove. The one thing she definitely did not love was getting ready in the morning.

"Angel," Mommy purred, "you have to get out of bed!"

"But it's so early!" Angel yowled. She covered her eyes with her paws. "Just a little bit longer?"

Mommy pulled off her daughter's seaweed blanket. "If you don't get up now, you'll be late meeting Coral and Shelly. You don't want to swim to sea school alone, do you?" she asked.

Angel pushed some fur out of her eyes and scowled. Mommy was right. She couldn't be late to see her best friends, Coral and Shelly. She loved exploring Kittentail Cove with them!

Angel was as bold as her black-and-white fur made her look. She was creative and daring, and loved making a splash. Shelly was a purrmaid with silky white fur, which she liked to keep purr-fectly clean. And orange kitten Coral could sometimes be a scaredy cat, which is why Angel loved helping her be brave!

As far back as Angel could remember, she had been friends with Shelly and Coral. It was hard to believe that three kittens who were so different inside and out could be such a good team. But they were! And Angel felt lucky to have two fin-tastic friends.

All three purrmaids were in the same class at sea school this year, and their teacher, Ms. Harbor, was paw-some.

Thinking of sea school made Angel smile. She twirled out of her oyster-shell bed. She stretched her paws up and her tail down.

She pulled on her new red top. Finally, she turned to the jewelry box on the table next to the bed.

Angel opened the lid and picked up her favorite bracelet. It had two beautiful charms on it—a golden seashell and a gold coin. Coral and Shelly had matching bracelets. They got the seashell charms to celebrate their friendship. They added the gold coins after they met Chomp the catshark in a shipwreck. Both charms reminded Angel of the fun adventures she'd had with her friends.

Her bracelet looked great, but Angel wanted more today. She put on a necklace made of angel wing shells. Then she grabbed the lavender pearl earrings that Mommy had given her on her birthday. She loved them. No one else she knew had earrings like that.

"Angel!" Mommy shouted. "Come and eat breakfast."

Angel rushed to the kitchen. Mommy held out a plate of seaweed pancakes and fish eggs. "My favorite!" Angel purred.

"Anything for my best kitten," Mommy replied. "Are you girls still coming to my office after sea school today?"

Angel nodded. "Shelly and Coral are really excited," she said. Mommy was on the Kittentail Cove Council. Her office was in Cove Council Hall. There was always something happening there. Today there was an extra treat for Angel and her friends. The council was getting a special tour of the Kittentail Cove Museum. Mommy was bringing Angel, Shelly, and Coral to the tour as her guests. Angel couldn't wait!

"See you this afternoon!" Angel said, kissing Mommy goodbye.

She swam to Leondra's Square and spotted flashes of white fur next to orange fur.

Coral and Shelly were already waiting for her.

"Angel!" Coral shouted. "We're going to be late!"

Angel giggled. Coral was always thinking about following the rules and not getting into trouble. "You don't have to worry about being late when you can swim fast!" she shouted. "I bet I can get there first!"

When the girls arrived at sea school, they hurried to room Eel-Twelve. As they swam through the classroom door, they saw the walls covered in posters. Each poster showed a different work of art from the Kittentail Cove Museum. "Wow!" Shelly purred.

"Do you like them?" Ms. Harbor asked.

Angel looked at her friends. "We love them!" she said.

"Wonderful!" Ms. Harbor said. "Then you will enjoy our art lesson today."

Angel grinned. Shelly loved cooking. Coral loved reading. But art was Angel's specialty! "This one was painted by Clawed Monet, right?" she asked, pointing. "And this is a Jackson Pawlock!"

"Slow down!" Ms. Harbor laughed. "Don't give away my lesson."

The bell rang, and the class took their seats. Ms. Harbor raised a paw. "Good morning, everyone," she said. "Today we are going to talk about art. We can learn a lot about purrmaid history from studying great artists and their masterpieces." She swam to one of the posters. "This is a painting by Pablo Picatso." She moved to the next one. "And this is a sculpture by Henri Catisse."

Someone behind Angel whispered, "I could do that." Angel looked over her shoulder to see who it was. It was a purrmaid named Adrianna.

The two girls sitting next to Adrianna giggled. Their names were Umiko and Cascade. Angel didn't know the other girls very well, but she knew that they were usually together doing the same things. They called themselves the Catfish Club.

Angel frowned. She didn't like anyone interrupting her teacher.

Umiko saw Angel's face and shushed her friends. The Catfish Club quieted down, and Angel was able to turn back to the lesson.

"Who knows why this artwork is special?" Ms. Harbor asked. When no one answered, she explained, "The artists didn't worry about what others told them to do. They didn't follow the rules. They followed their hearts! Their work helps the rest of us see the beauty in our world. Pay attention to what you like! For homework, I want you to work in groups to create your own masterpieces," she announced.

2

The class purred with excitement as soon as Ms. Harbor made her announcement.

Angel leaned toward Shelly and Coral. "We're all working together, right?" Angel whispered.

"Of course!" Coral laughed.

"I wouldn't want to work with anyone but you two," Shelly added.

Some students had questions. "Ms. Harbor, how are we supposed to do this homework?" Baker asked. "We're not real artists."

"And where are we supposed to get supplies?" Taylor added. He looked worried.

Ms. Harbor grinned. "First of all," she said, "each of you is *absolutely* a real artist! Whatever you create from your heart is real art. You don't need fish oil paint or squid ink brushes to make art! There are beautiful things all around us." She pointed to the ocean outside the classroom window. "Anything can be art."

The purrmaids in the class slowly nodded. Baker and Taylor looked more relaxed. But Angel wasn't feeling relaxed. She wasn't feeling worried, either. Angel was excited! "This is the best homework ever!" she whispered.

Normally, when Angel was that excited, it was hard for her to sit still and listen. But not while Ms. Harbor talked about all her favorite artists! When the bell rang, she was disappointed that the day was over!

Right after school, the girls headed to Cove Council Hall. Shelly and Coral struggled to keep up with Angel.

"Slow down, Angel!" Coral begged.

"Why are you speeding?" Shelly panted.

"The tour!" Angel replied. "I want to be the first ones to see the museum after the grand makeover!"

Everyone knew Angel loved being first. Winning, getting prizes, and being the best were all things that Angel tried hard to do. But going to the museum today wasn't just about winning. She thought they could brainstorm some good ideas for their homework from the museum.

Angel practically dragged Mommy out of her office. But when the four of them reached the front door of the museum, it was locked! Mommy looked at her watch. "The tour doesn't start for fifteen minutes," she explained. "We will have to wait."

"Rats!" Angel grumbled. All she wanted to do was to go inside.

"Let's get in line," Shelly suggested, "so we can be the first ones in."

"Great idea!" Angel agreed.

The girls lined up right in front of the museum. Slowly, other purrmaids gathered around the door, too. But the tour couldn't start without Mayor Rivers. "Where is the mayor?" Angel wondered, straining to see over the crowd of purrmaids.

Finally, she spied him. "We're going to be able to go in soon!" Angel squealed. She grabbed her friends' paws and danced around with happiness.

Mayor Rivers stopped near Mommy, and Angel's heart sank. He always talked for so long! Now they would have to wait again.

As she frowned at the talkative mayor, Angel didn't notice anyone swimming past. But then Shelly yowled, "Hey! You can't cut in front of us!"

It was the Catfish Club!

The three purrmaids didn't look alike. Adrianna's fur was silky and gray. Umiko's fur was white with orange and black patches. And Cascade's fur was a short cinnamon brown. But there was something about them that made them look like triplets.

After scowling for a moment, Angel realized what made the Catfish Club look so much alike. Each girl was wearing lavender. Their clothes were lavender. Their earrings were lavender. Their headbands were lavender. Even the pearl necklaces they wore were made from lavender pearls.

Lots of purrmaids had pearl jewelry. After all, they lived under the sea! But most pearls were white or black. Lavender pearls were very rare. That's what made Angel's earrings so special. She touched one of her earrings and thought, *There's no way three purrmaids would be wearing that much lavender on the same day without planning it ahead of time.*

Coral said, "You three need to get to the back of the line."

Umiko shrugged and started to swim away. But Adrianna grabbed her paw to stop her. "Was there a line?" she asked. She sounded innocent, but there was something fishy about the way she smiled.

Angel felt her face growing hot. She hissed, "Of course there was a line!"

"Actually," Cascade added, "this isn't a *line*. It's a crowd. So we can't really get to the back of the line."

Adrianna crossed her paws. "Besides," she shouted, "we're not going anywhere just because *you* tell us to!"

3

"My uncle is the mayor," Adrianna said, "and he said we could wait at the museum door."

"It doesn't matter what your uncle says!" Angel replied. "You have to wait your turn!"

Angel and Adrianna glared at each other. Coral and Shelly swam over and hovered next to Angel. They wanted to show the Catfish Club that they were on Angel's side. Cascade and Umiko did the same with

Adrianna. The two groups of girls stared each other down.

Angel was so mad she wanted to scream.

Mayor Rivers interrupted the staring contest. "Is there a problem?" he asked. Mommy swam behind him to see what was going on.

Angel went to Mommy's side. "Those three," she said, pointing at the Catfish Club, "cut in front of us."

Adrianna shook her head. "Uncle Ray," she said to Mayor Rivers, "we didn't know there was a line! We're just excited about the tour."

"I'm sure my niece and her friends didn't mean to cause trouble," Mayor Rivers said.

"We just want to be first," Umiko added.

The Catfish Club looked down at their tails like they were embarrassed. But Angel didn't believe it. "Well, we were here before you," she snapped. "And I like being first, too."

Angel tried to swim toward the other girls, but Mommy held her back. "It doesn't matter who is at the front of the line," Mommy purred. "We'll all be able to enjoy the artwork. Don't you agree, Angel?"

"Just let them go in," Shelly whispered into Angel's ear.

"We could get in trouble if we keep fighting!" Coral added. "We don't need to be first."

Angel didn't *need* to be first. But she enjoyed it. Just like she enjoyed winning and being the best. She really wanted to push those purrmaids out of line, but she knew her mother and her friends were right. Acting like the Catfish Club would make her just as bad as they were. She didn't like it, but she nodded anyway.

Luckily, Mrs. Clearwater, the director of the museum, opened the door. "Welcome to our special tour of Kittentail Cove Museum," she said. She steered everyone inside. Soon small groups of purrmaids swam off to explore the museum.

The Catfish Club went to the east wing of the museum. So Coral said, "We should go to the west wing!"

Angel stopped to look at a giant clamshell. The inside of the shell was splattered with different colors of fish oil paint. "It's the Jackson Pawlock painting from Ms. Harbor's poster!" she exclaimed.

Shelly tilted her head and squinted at the shell. "It's purr-ty," she said, "but he must have made a whale of a mess."

Angel giggled. Shelly hated to get her paws dirty! "Should we do something like this for our homework?" she teased.

Shelly shook her head and groaned.

Coral was on the other side of the gallery. She waved for her friends to come over. "Look at this one!" she shouted.

Coral hovered in front of a large canvas made from a sail from a shipwreck. It was a beautiful night scene of a town that looked a lot like Kittentail Cove. The moon and stars shone through the ocean and lit up the night sky.

"It's beautiful," Angel purred.

"Yes, it is," Mrs. Clearwater agreed. Angel turned around. The museum director was swimming beside Mommy. "It's one of my favorites," she continued. "Did you see what Vincent Fang Gogh used in this picture?"

Angel swam closer to the canvas. "It's not just paint," she gasped. "I see pearls and sea glass, too!"

Mrs. Clearwater nodded. "Exactly! Fang Gogh searched the ocean for things that would look like little strokes and spots of color. Up close, all you see are the spots. But swim away a bit," she explained, "and the spots come together to make a stunning starry night!"

"He was so creative!" Shelly said. "I never would have used pearls and sea glass."

"I thought you could only use paint," Coral added.

Mrs. Clearwater grinned. "Fang Gogh shows us how things that are lovely on their own can come together and create something even more special."

Mommy looked from Angel to Coral

to Shelly. "Just like the three of you are paw-some by yourselves, but when you get together, you're paw-sitively amazing!"

Angel gave Mommy a hug. She was right! Angel was smarter, braver, cooler, and more paw-some when Coral and Shelly were around!

Suddenly, Angel had an idea. "Mrs. Clearwater," she said, "we're supposed to create a piece of artwork for our homework tonight. Could we work on it here?"

"That's a great idea," Mommy agreed.

Mrs. Clearwater grinned. "Of course!"

The purrmaids followed Mrs. Clearwater through the halls of the museum. "I'll take you girls to the storage room," she said. "You can get inspiration from all the masterpieces that aren't on display right now. And there are lots of interesting things that you can use."

They swam past all the exhibits and soon reached a set of heavy double doors. The girls helped Mrs. Clearwater prop them open.

"Here you go," Mrs. Clearwater said. "You can work with anything you find in here!"

Angel smiled and led her friends inside. But what she saw made her freeze in place. "What is the Catfish Club doing here?" she sputtered.

4

"Do you girls know each other?" Mrs. Clearwater asked.

Angel rolled her eyes and muttered, "Unfortunately."

Coral nodded. "We're in the same class, Mrs. Clearwater," she answered.

"That's why you have the same homework!" Mrs. Clearwater said. "Have fun working together. Let me know if you need anything else."

As soon as Mrs. Clearwater was gone, Adrianna hissed, "You're being copycats."

"You heard us ask Mrs. Clearwater if we could work on our art project," Cascade added, "so you did, too?"

"Of course we didn't!" Coral exclaimed. "We didn't know you were going to be here. Angel had this idea all on her own."

The Catfish Club girls didn't look convinced.

"We were here first," Umiko said. "Maybe you guys should leave."

"We're not leaving!" Shelly yowled.

Angel sighed. She wanted to do their homework, not fight with the Catfish Club. "Maybe we should start over?" she suggested. "We're all in Ms. Harbor's class. We should at least try to be friends."

Umiko and Cascade nodded, but Adrianna crossed her paws. "You guys have been mean to us all afternoon," she said. "Why would we want to be friends?"

"Mean? Us?" Angel gasped. *They* were the ones who cut the line. *They* were the ones who were rude. *They* were the problem! "Oh, just forget it," she said. "You work on your project. We'll work on ours."

The Catfish Club began to swim away. Umiko stopped and looked back at Angel, Coral, and Shelly. "Let's try to stay out of each other's way," she suggested.

After Umiko left, Coral said, "I think she's right about steering clear of each other. I don't want to get into any trouble."

Angel led her friends in the opposite direction. They began searching for materials for their art project.

The museum's storage room was fintastic. Angel had never seen anything like it. It was as big as a blue whale! There were aisles of shelves that stretched back as far as she could see. "There's a lot here to explore!" she said.

"Look at this!" Coral shouted. She pointed to a row of statues on a high shelf. She swam next to one of a purrmaid perched on the edge of a rock, resting her chin on her paw. Coral copied the statue's pose. "Guess what I'm thinking!"

"I hope you're think-ing about our project!" Angel giggled.

Shelly joined in on the fun. She struck a pose with her chin up and her paws clasped behind her back. "Who am I?" she asked.

"The Kitten Dancer!" Angel cried. She swam to

the original statue on the lowest shelf. "One of my favorites!"

Angel could have spent the entire afternoon looking at all the statues, but that wasn't going to help with their homework! "Maybe we can come back to these if we finish our project," she said.

Shelly and Coral nodded. The girls moved to another set of shelves. This one didn't hold statues. Instead, there were large pieces of driftwood covered in bright, bold shapes.

"Do you know who painted these?" Coral asked.

Angel grinned. "Pablo Picatso!" she answered. "Remember how Ms. Harbor told us that anything can be art?" She pointed to some paintings. "Picatso used rectangles, circles, and zigzags to create these portraits."

"You know so much about art," Shelly said. "We're lucky to be working with you."

"Thank you!" Angel purred.

"I really like this," Coral said. She pointed to a painting of a purrmaid looking at her reflection in a mirror. "Do you think we should paint a portrait of Ms. Harbor?"

Angel's eyes lit up. "That is a paw-some idea!"

The purrmaids split up to find the supplies they needed. Coral found a bag filled with fish oil paints. Shelly picked up sea sponges, sea pens, and soft coral brushes.

But they needed something to paint on.

Angel scanned the aisles of the storage room, looking for something they could use as a canvas. She spied a giant sheet of seaweed paper. It was purr-fect! And it was big enough for two paintings in case they made a mistake.

Angel swam toward the paper. But just as she was about to reach for it, someone else's paws appeared. "This is paw-some!" a voice called out.

It was the Catfish Club, taking *her* paper!

5

Angel returned to her friends empty-handed. "I found a great piece of seaweed paper to use for our portrait," she explained, "but Adrianna got it before I did." She hung her head.

"Don't worry, Angel," Shelly said. "There have to be other things that would work."

Angel nodded, even though she was still upset.

The three purrmaids searched for something else to use for their project. "How about that?" Coral asked, pointing at a flat rock.

Angel shook her head. "It's too heavy," she said. "We'd need more paws to help carry it out of the museum."

"You're right," Coral agreed.

They went back to their search. But instead of finding something lighter, the purrmaids found the Catfish Club. They seemed to be on the hunt for something, too.

"I wonder what they're looking for," Angel whispered.

Shelly and Coral shrugged. "I don't know," Shelly said, "but maybe we should go the other way."

They tried to turn around quietly and swim away before they were seen, but it wasn't their lucky day. Adrianna spotted them and shouted, "Hey! Are you spying on us?"

Angel spun around to face the Catfish Club. "Of course not," she snapped. "We're looking for something to paint a portrait on."

"We already found this," Adrianna said, holding up the seaweed paper.

"But we haven't found any paints," Umiko added.

"Or brushes," Cascade said. "Not even a sea sponge!"

"We found paint," Coral said, "and a whole bunch of sponges and brushes."

Adrianna's eyes narrowed. "Did you three take all the supplies?" she asked. "I'm telling! Wait until my uncle the mayor hears about this!"

"We took what we found," Shelly replied, "like Mrs. Clearwater said we could."

"You didn't leave brushes for anyone else to use," Umiko said.

"And you three didn't leave seaweed paper for us, either," Angel snapped.

"Well, what are we supposed to do now?" Cascade asked.

Angel glanced at Shelly and Coral. She had an idea. She just couldn't believe what she was about to say.

Angel pulled her friends toward her. She wanted to talk to them without the other girls hearing. "We can't do our project without paper," she whispered. "And they can't do their project without paints and tools. We're all stuck, unless . . ." She paused and bit her lip.

Shelly finished Angel's sentence. "Unless we share."

Coral agreed. "I think that makes sense," she said. "I don't want to get in trouble if we don't finish our homework."

"So it's decided?" Angel asked.

Her friends nodded.

Angel held the fish oil paint and brushes out to the Catfish Club. "If you guys will share your seaweed paper," she said, "then we'll share our supplies."

"I thought of that already," Cascade purred. "I was going to suggest it, too. It's the best plan."

"I vote yes," Umiko added.

After a moment, Adrianna shrugged. "I guess we can do that," she agreed.

The girls split up the supplies, and then carefully cut the seaweed paper in half. Soon each group had everything they needed.

"I can't wait to actually *start* on this project!" Angel exclaimed.

Then she overheard the Catfish Club's conversation. Umiko said, "Let's go, girls. We can finally get to work!"

"It's going to be so paw-some," Cascade said.

"The best in the whole class," Adrianna added.

Angel couldn't hold back. "The best in the class?" she snorted.

"Ignore them," Coral whispered. "It's not a contest." She tried to pull her friend away.

Angel frowned. Coral was right. It really wasn't a contest. But even when no one else was competing, Angel hated to lose! "I bet it won't be the best," she shouted.

"What?" Umiko asked.

"I said," Angel answered, "I bet your project won't be the best in the class."

"Really?" Cascade asked. "What would you bet?"

Angel paused for a moment. She knew she was getting too upset, but she couldn't help herself. She yelled, "I would bet *anything* that Ms. Harbor likes what we make more than whatever you three come up with!"

Adrianna's eyes narrowed. "Would you

bet those earrings?" she hissed.

Angel's paw went right to one of her pearls. "What?" she yelped.

Umiko swam between Adrianna and Angel. "Let's stop this," she said. "Someone is going to say something she doesn't mean—"

But Adrianna cut Umiko off. "You said you'd bet anything," she said to Angel. "We want to bet your earrings."

Angel didn't want to risk losing her lavender pearl earrings. Her friends knew it, too. Shelly whispered, "Angel, you love those earrings. This bet isn't worth it."

"Let's just go," Coral suggested.

Angel was about to nod when Adrianna said, "We get it. You're just a chicken in the sea."

"Actually," Cascade whispered, "chickens don't live in the ocean. So she couldn't really be a chicken in the sea."

Adrianna elbowed Cascade to be quiet. Coral and Shelly tried to hide their mouths with their paws so no one would see them giggling. But Angel didn't pay attention to Cascade's funny fact. She clenched her jaw so much that it hurt. Then she shouted, "You want to make a bet? Fine! What are you going to give us when our project is better than yours?"

That made the Catfish Club quiet down. They looked at each other. Then Cascade said, "Your earrings match our necklaces, so if Ms. Harbor likes your art better, we'll give you one. But if she likes what we make more, then you give us your earrings."

Angel ignored the looks on her friends' faces and declared, "It's a bet. May the best artists win!"

6

Shelly and Coral yanked Angel away from the Catfish Club almost immediately.

"What did you do, Angel?" Coral cried. "You can't give them your earrings!"

"What would your mother say if you lost them?" Shelly added. "It would be a cat-tastrophe!"

"You would get in so much trouble!" Coral gasped. "In fact, you might even get *us* in trouble!"

"Relax!" Angel replied. "There's no way they can do a better job than we can."

Coral and Shelly shook their heads. "We hope you're right, Angel," Coral said.

Angel waved her friends over to a table in a corner of the storage room. "Let's get to work," she said. They cleared the table off, and Angel carefully unrolled the seaweed paper. Shelly found an oyster-shell palette and carefully squeezed different colors of paint onto it. Coral arranged the brushes and sponges on the table.

"How should we start?" Shelly asked.

Coral shrugged. "I've never painted a portrait before," she admitted, "or used fish oil paint."

Angel hadn't, either. But how hard could it be? She picked up a sponge and dunked it in some green paint. "I guess we can start with the background," she suggested. She started to swab the paint across the paper.

"That looks great!" Shelly commented.

Angel smiled. "Thanks!" She put the sponge down and dipped a brush in black paint. She started to paint a circle for Ms. Harbor's face. But when Angel pulled the brush along the seaweed paper, something terrible happened. "Rats!" she yelped.

"What is it?" Coral asked.

Angel moved the brush aside and pointed. "The paper ripped!" she cried.

Coral and Shelly examined the tear. "It isn't so bad," Shelly said. She softly pushed the edges of the paper down. "Let's just be more careful."

"I was being gentle, I promise!" Angel said.

"We know, Angel," Coral soothed.

Angel held the brush out to Shelly and Coral. "Maybe one of you should try," she suggested. "I don't want to make it worse."

Shelly picked up the brush and dipped it into the paint. Then she lightly brushed it against the seaweed paper. She finished the circle.

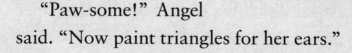

"Paw-some!" Angel said. "Now paint triangles for her ears."

Shelly nodded and turned to the paper again. She carefully painted one ear. But when she lifted the brush off to get more paint, a chunk of the paper stuck to it and tore off!

"I'm sorry!" Shelly yowled. Before, there was just a little tear in the seaweed paper. Now there was a hole where Ms. Harbor's ear should be.

"It isn't your fault," Coral said. She put a paw around Shelly's shoulders. "The same thing happened to Angel."

Angel nodded. "Coral is right. I guess we just don't know how to work with seaweed paper and fish oil paint."

"Maybe we could cut off a smaller piece and start over?" Coral suggested.

Angel shook her head. "I think the paper is too thin," she said. "It wasn't the best idea to try to paint on it. Especially since we've never done it before."

"What are we going to do now?" Shelly asked. "You need a project that can win your bet with the Catfish Club."

Angel bit her lip. *I wish I hadn't lost my temper and made that bet,* she thought. There was no way Ms. Harbor would think a portrait filled with rips and tears was the better project. She felt butterfly fish fluttering in her tummy.

"Should we search for more supplies?" Coral wondered. "There has to be something here we know how to use."

"I guess," Angel said. "We don't really have a choice. And we can look for a trash can, too." She crumpled up the seaweed paper. "This is just garbage now."

The girls nodded sadly. They began

to swim down the aisles again. They saw many more beautiful pieces of art, but they couldn't find any other art supplies.

Angel spied a trash can at the end of an aisle. "Let's get rid of this," she said, holding up the ball of seaweed paper. Her friends followed her down the aisle.

Before they reached the trash can, Angel heard something. "What's that?" she asked.

Shelly shrugged.

Coral said, "It sounds like someone is upset."

They poked their heads around a corner to see where the noise was coming from.

It was the Catfish Club! They were all crying!

Angel squirmed. She didn't like seeing other purrmaids in tears, even when they got on her nerves. "Should we find out what's wrong?" she asked.

"I think that's the right thing to do," Coral said.

Shelly nodded.

The girls slowly approached the Catfish Club. Angel tapped Adrianna's shoulder and asked, "Are you guys all right?"

The Catfish Club flinched at Angel's
voice. They wiped their faces with their
paws and turned around. "Did you come to
make fun of us?" Adrianna spat.

"No!" Angel said. "We're just worried
about you."

"What happened?" Shelly asked.

Umiko pointed to the table behind them.
"I guess Angel is going to win the bet," she
said. "Our painting is ruined!"

"We kept ripping holes in the paper," Cascade added, "no matter what we tried."

"And now we don't have an art project at all!" Adrianna cried. She ripped their paper in half over and over until it was just a pile of scraps.

Angel looked down at the crumpled ball in her own paw. They'd all had the same problem. And now they were all in the same mess. No one had homework to bring in tomorrow.

Maybe the Catfish Club isn't so different from us after all, Angel thought. She held out her paw and said, "You guys should know that you didn't do anything wrong."

"Our paper ripped when we tried to paint on it, too," Shelly added.

"I told you seaweed paper is tricky," Cascade sobbed.

The Catfish Club sniffled and glanced at each other. "So you don't have a project, either?" Umiko asked.

Angel, Coral, and Shelly shook their heads. "We're in deep trouble, just like you," Coral said.

"What are you going to do?" Cascade asked. "We don't have any more ideas. *I* can't even think of something!"

"And we don't have a lot of time left," Adrianna added. "Uncle Ray will be taking us home soon."

"We're going to leave soon, too," Shelly said.

The six purrmaids looked down at their tails. Everyone seemed frustrated and a little sad.

Angel remembered how excited she'd been about this homework. *Now it's a cat-tastrophe,* she thought. Her eyes teared up, but she didn't want to cry in front of everyone. So she grabbed the pile of scraps and swam over to the trash can. She lifted the lid to throw away both pieces of ruined seaweed paper.

But when Angel looked inside, her eyes grew wide. "Come here!" she shouted. "Everybody, come here right now!"

"What is it?" Coral asked. She and the others swam swiftly to Angel's side.

Angel pointed to the trash can. "Just look!" she said.

The purrmaids peeked inside. "It's filled with garbage," Adrianna said, confused. "Why are you so excited about trash?"

There was always garbage in Kittentail Cove. Some was created by purrmaids in their daily lives. But there was also rubbish that floated into the cove from human ships and beaches. Keeping their town clean was a way to keep Kittentail Cove purr-ty, but it also

kept sea animals safe. No one in the ocean wanted turtles or seals or birds to accidentally eat a piece of garbage that could harm them.

There were trash cans all over the cove to make it easy to tidy up every last corner. The things that got thrown away looked ugly littering the streets of the town, but that didn't mean they were *always* ugly.

"Anything can be art," Angel said. She grabbed the trash can and dumped the contents on the floor. "We've been thinking about this the wrong way. We don't need fancy paints or papers." She grabbed a metal bottle cap from the pile of garbage. "Look at how shiny this is," she said. "A bunch of these could look like stars shining on a clear ocean night." Then she picked up a handful of sea glass pieces and broken seashells. "And look at how colorful these are. I see all the shades of the buildings of Kittentail Cove."

Umiko reached for a piece of a white plastic wrapper. Humans used things like that to wrap around something they called candy. "This could be cut to look like a moon," she suggested.

"But, Angel," Shelly complained, "it's garbage! It's so dirty!"

"We would make sure everything is clean," Angel explained. She leaned toward Shelly and whispered, "I know you don't like getting dirty."

Shelly smiled at her friend. Then Coral exclaimed, "Angel, you figured it out! We can use these things to make our own *Starry Night* picture!"

Coral and Shelly pulled Angel into a bear hug. "Unless the Catfish Club comes up with a new idea," Coral whispered, "you'll win the bet!"

"Your earrings are safe!" Shelly added.

Out of the corner of her eye, Angel saw the other purrmaids' shoulders slump and their eyes lower. As much as she wanted to win their bet, she knew what she had to do next.

Angel pulled away from her friends and swam toward the Catfish Club. "I think we should—" she began. She paused to take a deep breath before continuing. "I think we should work together."

"All six of us?" Cascade gasped.

Angel nodded. "We're all in the same class. We all want to do a good job." She glanced at the scraps of seaweed paper in the litter pile. "We're all terrible fish oil artists," she joked.

The other girls giggled.

"If we work together," Angel declared, "I know we can create a masterpiece."

8

In an instant, the six purrmaids were smiling and energized. They zipped off in all directions to gather the rest of what they would need.

"I've got snail slime!" Coral shouted. "We can use it as glue."

"We found these," Cascade said. She and Umiko held up a bag of coral pieces.

"I think these are the leftovers from sculpting a coral statue," Umiko said.

"They remind me of the view of Tortoiseshell Reef from Cove Council Hall," Cascade said.

Umiko held up one of the coral pieces. "This one looks a little bit like the statue in Leondra's Square." She giggled.

Angel beamed. "This is great!" she exclaimed.

Shelly and Adrianna swam over. "I think we found the perfect canvas for our *Starry Night*," Shelly said.

"Follow us!" Adrianna said.

The two girls led everyone to the flat rock Coral had found earlier. Angel scrunched her brow. "But it's too heavy!" she said.

Shelly and Adrianna shook their heads. "It was too heavy for the three of you," Adrianna said, "but like my uncle the mayor likes to say, '*When purrmaids work together, anything is possible!*' With six pairs of paws, we should be strong enough to do anything we want!"

"You're right!" Angel laughed.

The purrmaids arranged their discoveries next to the rock. Coral painted the entire surface blue. "Finally, no rips!" she joked.

Shelly and Umiko glued the shells and sea glass into the shape of Cove Council Hall on one side of the project, while Angel created sea school on the other. Adrianna used the coral pieces to make Tortoiseshell Reef. Cascade used a sharp claw to slice the candy wrapper into a crescent moon. And they all worked together to glue the bottle cap stars onto the blue sky.

As they passed the bottle of snail slime back and forth, Umiko said, "You know, we really didn't mean to cut the line earlier."

Cascade nodded. "We just weren't paying attention."

"And then you guys were so angry," Adrianna said, "that we reacted badly."

Angel felt her face grow hot. "I'm sorry for snapping," she said.

"We are, too," Coral and Shelly echoed.

"We all got off on the wrong paw," Angel said. "I'm glad we started over."

The purrmaids smiled at each other. Then Angel glued the last bottle cap on. "I think we're done!" she purred.

Everyone floated back to take a good look at their project.

"It doesn't look like the Fang Gogh painting," Adrianna said.

"That's because Fang Gogh never saw Kittentail Cove!" Shelly laughed.

"I think this looks paw-some," Coral said.

"Paw-sitively amazing," Umiko added.

"I agree," Cascade said. Then she turned

to Angel. "Thank you for suggesting that we all work together."

"We were actually ready to give up," Adrianna said.

"We couldn't have done this without you," Umiko said. "Or you and you," she added to Coral and Shelly.

Angel grinned. "Well, we couldn't have done it without you, either. But now we really do need each other. Everybody grab an edge. Let's get this thing home!"

The girls lifted the rock. Even with six of them, it was very heavy. "This is harder than I thought it would be," Adrianna panted.

"Don't think about it," Coral answered. "Just lift and swim!"

They carefully passed through the double doors and then down the hallway.

By the time they reached the museum entryway, they were huffing and puffing. "Let's take a break," Angel suggested.

She didn't have to tell the other purrmaids twice! They propped the rock against the wall and sat down on the floor to rest.

"What do you have there?" someone asked.

Angel turned around. "Mommy!" she cried. She leapt up to hug her mother. "Look at our art project!"

Mayor Rivers and Mrs. Clearwater swam over to look, too. When Mrs. Clearwater saw the creation, her paw went to her heart. "This is incredible, girls!" she said.

"Is this . . . is this *Starry Night*?" Mommy asked.

Angel grinned and said, "I think we would call it *Starry Kittentail Cove*."

"Did you make this out of things from our storeroom?" Mrs. Clearwater asked.

"Yes!" Cascade said. "We found this rock on a shelf and thought it would be perfect as a canvas."

"We used fish oil paint for the background," Umiko said.

"Then Angel had the idea to use things we found in the trash can," Adrianna said. She pointed to the bottle caps and the broken shells and sea glass. "It was a paw-some plan."

"I'm very impressed," Mrs. Clearwater said. "You girls accomplished something that many artists spend their lives trying to do. You saw the beauty in things that get overlooked and found ways to share that beauty with everyone else."

"I'm proud of you," Mommy said, "especially since all *six* of you figured out a way to work together."

The purrmaids beamed. "Now we just have to carry this home," Angel purred.

Mrs. Clearwater blocked their path. "You can't do that," she said, frowning.

"But you said we could use the storeroom stuff for our project!" Angel yelped.

Mrs. Clearwater nodded. "Yes, I did," she said. "And I'm amazed at what you created. But you can't take that out of the museum." She swam to the front entrance. "It's too big to fit through our new door!"

The purrmaids didn't want to believe it. They tried to get the rock through the front door. But no matter how they twisted or turned, their project was too tall and wide.

"I'm so sorry, girls," Mrs. Clearwater purred. "That rock has been in the storage room fur-ever. We did repairs to the museum and replaced the old double doors with this one." She shrugged. "We never thought we'd need to move something that size!"

"What are we going to do about our homework?" Adrianna whined. "Do something, Uncle Ray! You're the *mayor*!"

"I can speak to Ms. Harbor," Mayor Rivers said. "I'll explain what happened. I'm sure she'll understand."

"I'll talk to her, too," Mommy added. "Let's get you girls home, and then I can call her shell phone."

The purrmaids were as quiet as a clam while they swam home. Angel waved goodbye when they dropped off Shelly and Coral but couldn't bring herself to speak.

In the morning, when it was time to get ready for school, Angel was more miserable than usual. She wanted the day to be over before it even started.

"Come on, Angel," Mommy purred. "I told you I talked to Ms. Harbor. She understands what happened."

Angel squeezed her eyes shut and turned her face away. "I still don't want to go to school," she mumbled.

"You *still* have to go," Mommy replied.

Angel, Coral, and Shelly were mostly silent on the swim to sea school. The students in room Eel-Twelve weren't silent, though. Ms. Harbor wasn't in the classroom yet, but everyone else was there. And except for the Catfish Club, everyone else had their art projects.

Some purrmaids had made a sand sculpture of sea school. Another group made a seaweed collage of swimming dolphins.

Baker and Taylor used pages out of an old human book to fold into a collection of shells.

The Catfish Club girls were sitting quietly at their desks. Angel led Shelly and Coral over to them. "Ours was just as good as these," she whispered.

The other girls nodded. "Too bad no one will see it," Umiko mumbled.

"Can I have everyone's attention, please?" Ms. Harbor asked. The purrmaids took their seats. "I know you just got here," she continued, "but we're not staying in class. We have a special appointment this morning!"

"What about our projects?" Baker asked.

"Where are we going?" Taylor asked.

"You'll each get to present your creations," Ms. Harbor said, smiling, "*after* we get back from Kittentail Cove Museum."

Angel's heart sank. That was the last place in the ocean she wanted to go!

When she glanced around, most of the students were smiling. But Shelly, Coral, Adrianna, Umiko, and Cascade all had the same look on their faces—upside-down smiles.

As the class lined up, Angel whispered, "Why do we have to go back to the museum?" Her friends shrugged.

The trip through Kittentail Cove seemed to take forever. Ms. Harbor had to remind Angel to keep up. "I've never seen you swim so slowly!" she said.

Mrs. Clearwater was waiting at the entrance of the museum. "Welcome," she said. "I'm Mrs. Clearwater, the museum director. Ms. Harbor asked me to help with your art lesson today."

"There are so many things you can explore at Kittentail Cove Museum," Ms. Harbor said, "but today we are here to see one thing in particular."

"Follow me," Mrs. Clearwater said. She led the class into the next gallery.

As soon as Angel swam into the room, she froze. "Is that . . . ," she whispered.

Coral and Shelly swam up behind her. Their mouths opened and closed, but nothing came out.

Then the Catfish Club came in. Their eyes grew wide. Adrianna finally broke the silence. "Is that what I think it is?" she asked.

Ms. Harbor and Mrs. Clearwater hovered on either side of a large flat rock. It had been hung in the gallery alongside paintings by Fang Gogh, Picatso, and Furmeer. But the picture on the rock hadn't been created by a famous artist.

"Yesterday, some of your classmates came here to do their homework assignment," Mrs. Clearwater said. "Unfortunately, the project was too big to remove from the museum." She smiled. "But that just means we get to keep this beautiful work by these local Kittentail Cove artists right here on our wall!" She swam over to Angel, Coral, Shelly, and the Catfish Club.

"You guys made this?" Baker asked. "It looks like Kittentail Cove."

"It's fin-tastic!" Taylor added.

"A true masterpiece!" Ms. Harbor declared.

10

"Before you return to sea school," said Mrs. Clearwater, "take a few moments to look through the gallery at the other artwork."

The students happily swam off in all directions, except the six creators of *Starry Kittentail Cove*. They hovered in the same place, staring at their creation.

"I can't believe our work is in a *real* museum," Angel purred.

"That's because it's *real* art." Ms. Harbor laughed. "When Mrs. Shore and Mayor Rivers told me about the size of your problem, I knew there had to be something we could do."

"Then I had the idea to place your work exactly where it belongs!" Mrs. Clearwater said.

"I have a question," Ms. Harbor said. "I'm surprised that the six of you decided to work together. When you left class yesterday, I thought you'd be in two groups of three."

Angel bit her lip. She looked at Coral and Shelly first, and then over at the Catfish Club. No one wanted to be the first to talk, so Angel took a deep breath. "I think I can explain," she began. "Shelly, Coral, and I were planning to work as a group."

"And Umiko, Adrianna, and I were going to work as our own group," Cascade added.

Angel nodded. "We were all here yesterday, and we got a little . . . competitive," she explained.

"Our claws may have come out." Umiko giggled.

"We were working against each other until things got completely out of paw," Angel continued. "But then we realized that what we could make together—"

"Was better than what we could accomplish alone!" Adrianna declared.

Ms. Harbor smiled at them. "You girls learned a great lesson," she said.

"That's because we have a great teacher!" Angel laughed.

"Now, girls, finish admiring your work," Mrs. Clearwater purred. "You have to get back to school soon."

The purrmaids nodded. As soon as the grown-ups were too far away to hear, Angel let out a squeal of delight. "Ms. Harbor loved *Starry Kittentail Cove*!" she exclaimed.

"I was thinking the same thing!" Coral said.

"Me too!" Shelly added.

The Catfish Club girls, though, didn't answer. They were off to the side, whispering to each other. When they finally swam over, they weren't smiling.

"We have to talk to you," Adrianna said.

"We have a bet to settle," Cascade added.

"What?" Angel said, confused. "We worked together!"

"How can there still be a bet?" Shelly asked.

Umiko held up a paw. "We just talked about it, and we think there's a pretty clear winner here."

"Angel, you're the reason we even have a project to show today," Adrianna said.

"Your idea was the best," Umiko added, "so you win."

"The three of you didn't need to let us work with you," Cascade said. "You could have created *Starry Kittentail Cove* without our help."

Angel shook her head, but Adrianna stopped her. "Cascade is right," she said.

"I'm right a lot." Cascade giggled.

"We want you guys to have these," Umiko explained.

Each girl took a pearl off her necklace and held it out.

"There's one for each of you," Cascade said. "We thought maybe you could wear them on your bracelets."

Angel looked from Coral to Shelly. She was so surprised! "I don't know what to say," she mumbled.

Adrianna giggled. "As my uncle the mayor would say, '*Just say, Thank you.*' "

Angel, Coral, and Shelly each clipped the lavender pearls to their bracelets. "Thank you," Shelly purred. Coral and Angel nodded.

"You guys were the best this time," Umiko admitted.

"We'll see what happens next time," Cascade added.

"Yes, we will!" Angel laughed. She knew there would be a next time with the Catfish Club—and she was looking forward to it!

Francesco Quaglia

Sudipta Bardhan-Quallen

has never met a mermaid, but she did have three cats in college. She is the author of many books for young readers, including *Duck, Duck, Moose!*; *Chicks Run Wild*; *Hampire*; and *Snoring Beauty*. She lives in New Jersey with her family and an imaginary pony named Penny.

Vivien Wu

has illustrated several books with Random House and Disney Publishing, including five Little Golden Books. She also has an online shop, where she creates more artwork populated by purrmaids and feline-folk. She lives in Los Angeles with her cat, Mimi.